Old King Stinky Toes

Baxter Owen Graham
and my dad
Illustrated By James R. Martin

Historical Note

During the winter of 2000 – my then 7 year old son Baxter and I began the legend of Old King Stinky Toes. Some months later we completed the fictional account and I chronicled the story in the hard drive of an old laptop. And that's where it stayed until the fall of 2004 when I decided to make it a collective work between a father, his son, and his fourth grade teacher. We painstakingly reworked the original story into rhyme, developed the characters, and learned more than we wanted to know about publishing children's books. But the memorable tale and the entirety of the experience brought a father, his son and his teacher to depths of laughter and imagination. Illustrator James Martin was Baxter's fourth grade elementary teacher and mentor. His fun and creative energy is distinctive and inspired. The three of us have created a new media company to further our creative gremlins.

—Robert H. Graham

Drumstick Media
A division of Old Goats, Inc.
5805 Highway 93 South, Whitefish
Montana 59937

Text Copyright © 2005
by Baxter Owen Graham
Illustrations Copyright © 2005
by James R. Martin

Published by Drumstick Media

Book design by Robert H. Graham and James R. Martin

The illustrations are rendered in color pencil, charcoal and pen and ink

Old King Stinky Toes/ by Baxter Owen Graham; illustrated by James R. Martin

First Edition

Summary: His stinky toes champion the hero's courage by driving a bumbling dragon away from his terrorized kingdom. The Kings subjects come to realize, "It's not what's on the outside that counts, it's what's on the inside. The King serves others with his courage wisdom and heart."

ISBN: 0-9764791-0-9

Library of Congress Catalog Card Number 2005900270

Printed in the USA

Special Thanks and Dedication to:

Laughter and Imagination

Main Characters

Old King Stinky Toes
Bumblegump the Dragon

Supporting Cast

Ian Squillhead   Phillip Proboscis
Jacobius Jester   Patrick Pachyderm
Francine Filibuster   Caufus Clauser

Knights

Sir Perfluous   Sir Lancenot   Sir Furthur
Sir Wantmydad   Sir Imfaint   Sir Jamama
Sir MaryKay   Sir Bors tu tears   Sir Bedfear
                     Sir Trystan de cat

Friends

Kolbe my Dog   Cheesecake my Rat

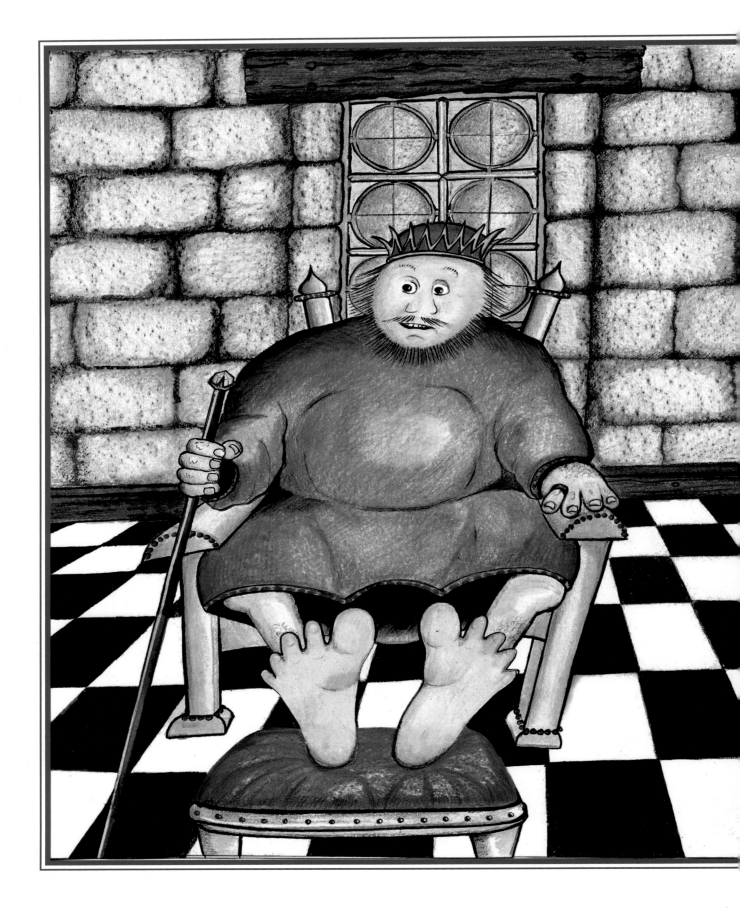

Old King Stinky Toes
was a very stinky man . . .

He was a good and kind king,
but his subjects made him sad!

Although he was kindhearted,
it really didn't matter.

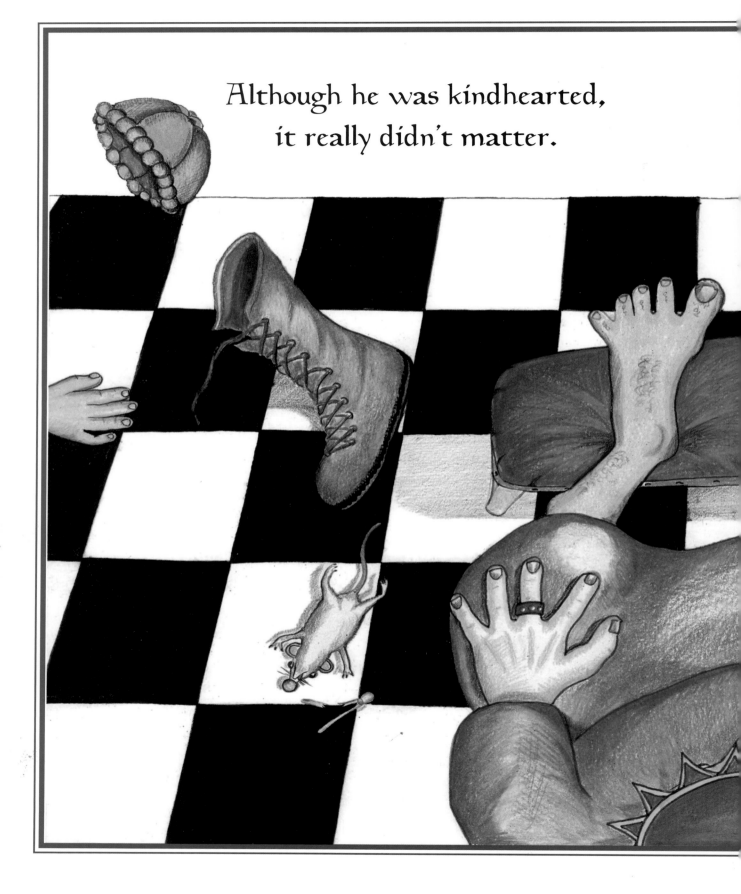

For when he took his shoes off,
his subjects they would scatter.

They'd say such dreadful things to him about his stinky toes.

They'd throw rotten food and eggs at him wherever he would go.

At first it made him very scared,
and then it made him mad.

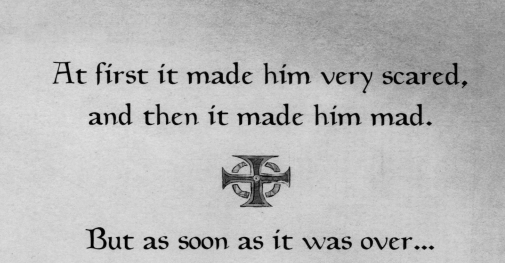

But as soon as it was over...
He felt so awfully sad!

One dark day a bumbling dragon
destroyed the village square.

He smashed their houses down to dust;
'twas more than they could bear!

They held their noses, wheezed and coughed,
and gathered on the brink.

"What will you do," they begged and pleaded,
"Old King with toes that stink?"

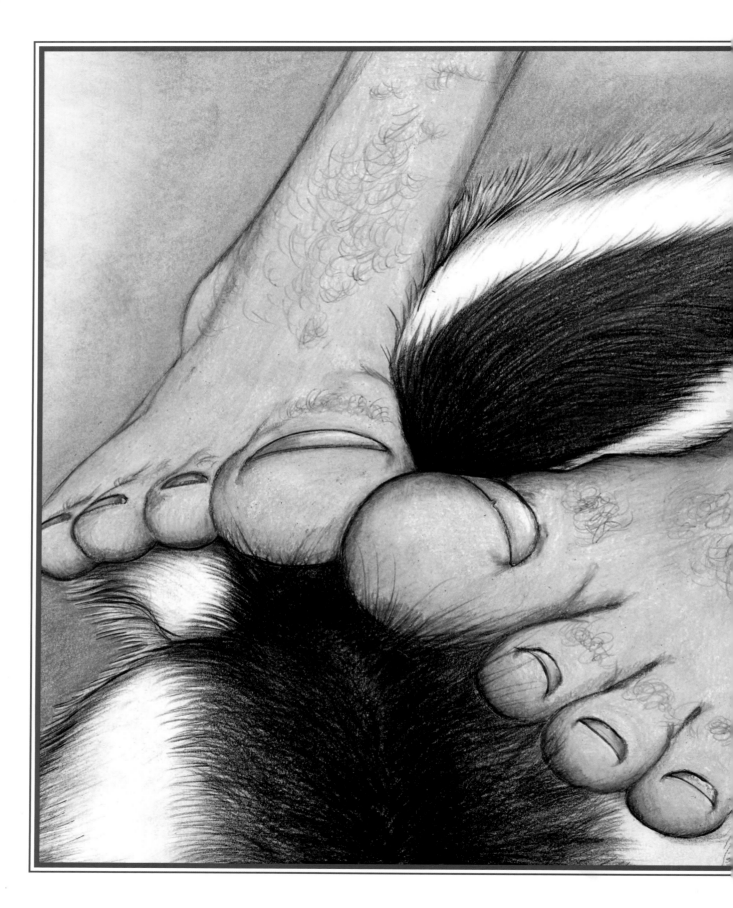

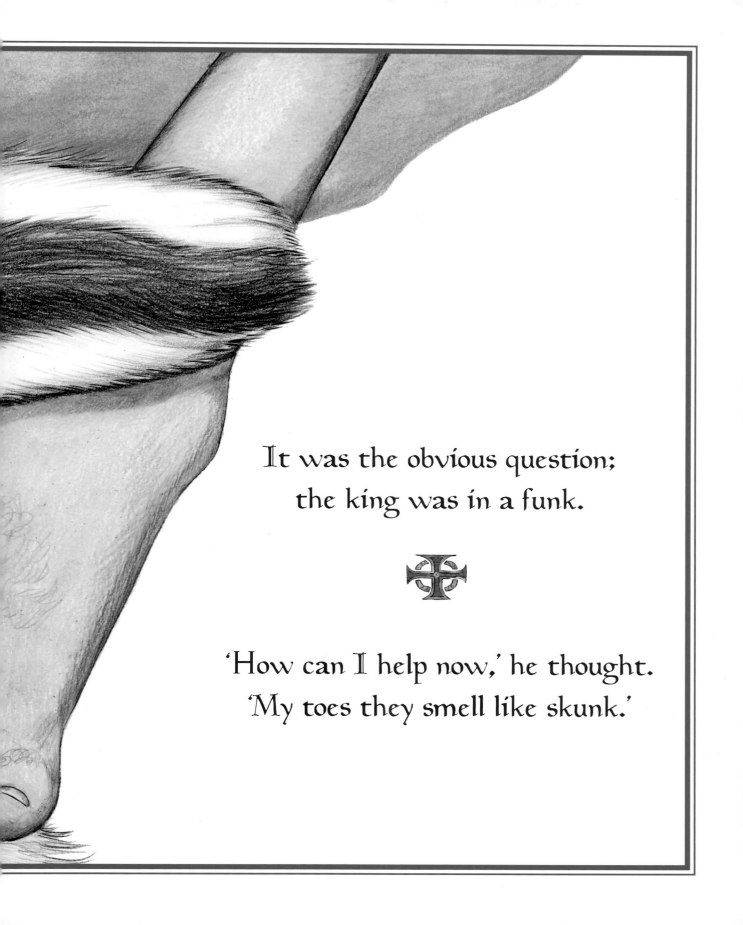

It was the obvious question;
the king was in a funk.

'How can I help now,' he thought.
'My toes they smell like skunk.'

He hailed his knights
and soon they gathered
at the table round.

And swiftly he decided,
"They'll slay this
dragon down."

But soon they were defeated,
he no longer could postpone.

He knew this dragon must be slain;
he'd do it on his own.

The king prepared for battle
and gathered up his might.

He put on all his armor;
he was ready for the fight.

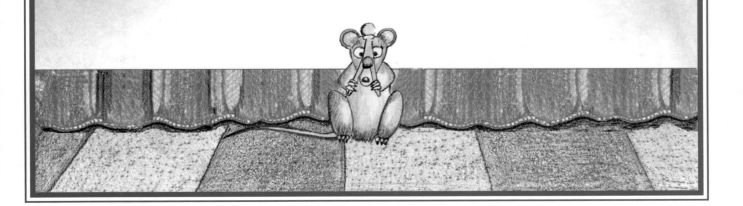

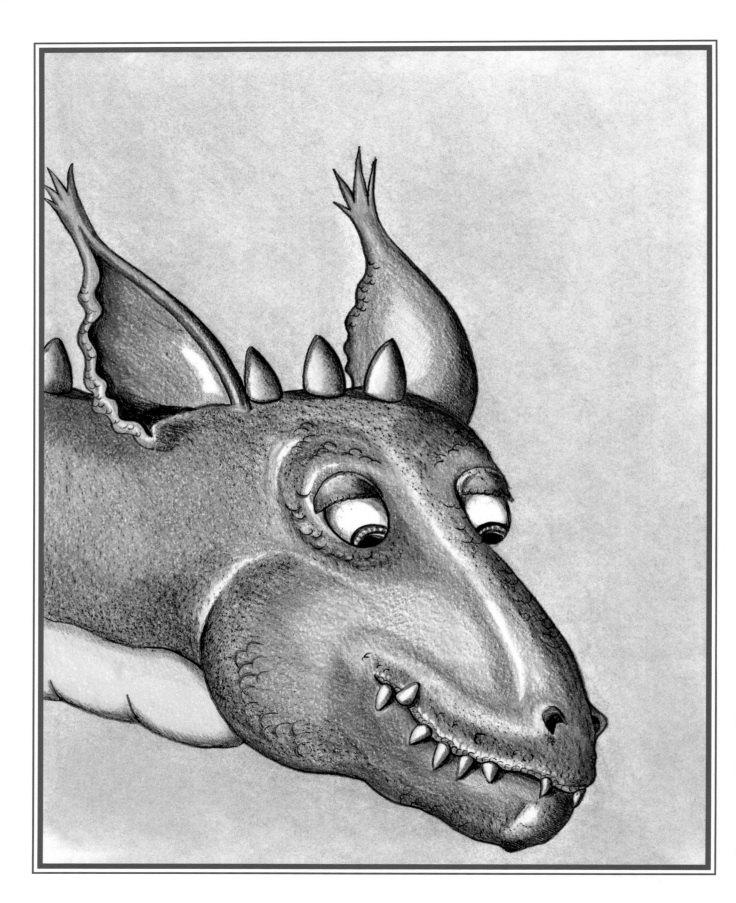

When he found the bumbling dragon,
he knew it wasn't good.

His knees were knocking wildly;
he'd flee now if he could.

Happily he remembered
why his servants were so rude.

He smelled a disgusting odor,
his courage was renewed.

He sneaked up on the dragon,
and sat upon a bench.

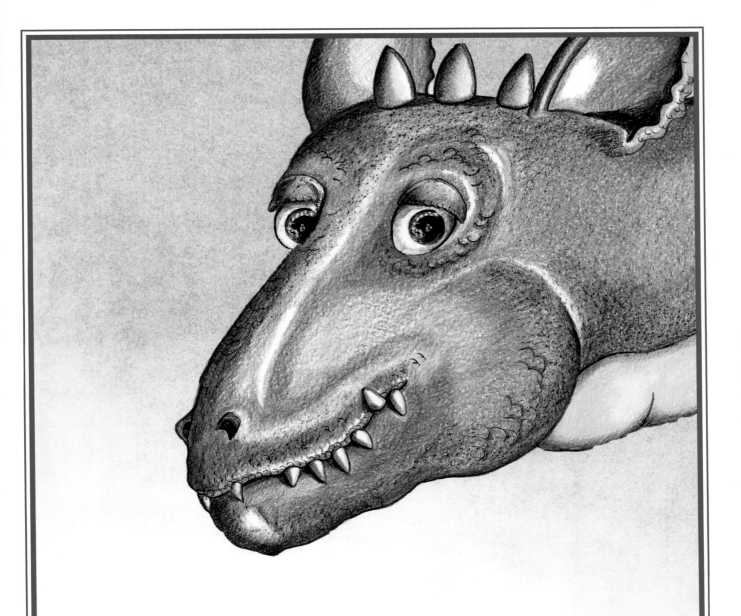

He removed his boots and holey socks
and freed the awful stench!

The dragon's eyes began to wilt;
he sneezed, then choked and coughed.

The cloud of stink had done him in,
he'd soon set sail aloft.

The town was saved,
the king was loved;
they cheered his very name.
The King became a legend; though
his toes stink just the same.